A Different Kind of Christmas Story

ISBN: 9781020001352 (Paperback)
First Edition

10 9 8 7 6 5 4 3 2

45 Alternate Press, LLC
www.45alternate.com

A Different Kind of Christmas Story

A Carol in 100-Word Stories

Ran Walker

Contents

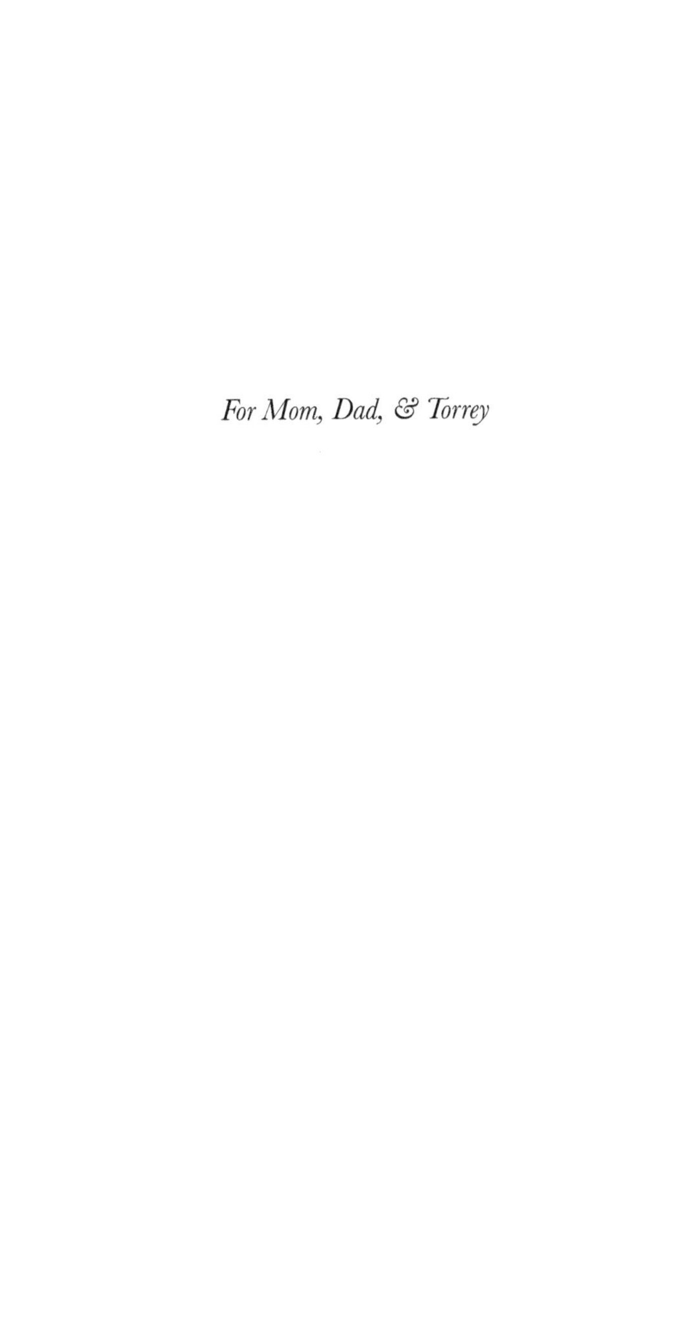

For Mom, Dad, & Torrey

The children were nestled all snug in their beds, while visions of sugar-plums danced in their heads…

— Clement Clarke Moore

December 1983
Daily, Mississippi

Once upon a time in a small town...

Chapter 1
Daily, Mississippi

Once listed in a national periodical as one of the 100 most beautiful towns in America, Daily, Mississippi, believed in doing Christmas big. *Norman Rockwell big!*

Lights lined the store windows on Main Street, tinsel Christmas trees and holiday bells affixed to the tops of street lamps.

The park in the center of town housed candy canes, reindeer cutouts, and snowmen made of plaster, all surrounding a gazebo illuminated in red and green lights.

And all the grudges people held against each other during the year were set aside, a reprieve to embrace the magic and beauty of the season.

Chapter 2
The Parkers of Elm Street

ANDERSON SR. HADN'T ORIGINALLY PLANNED to put lights on the house, but his neighbors had already started the usual decoration wars. Although the Parker family was one of three Black families on a predominately white Elm Street, Anderson Sr. refused to have his neighbors looking down their noses at him.

As a dentist, he found himself always meticulously concerned about his smile. He kept it large and unthreatening, traits that he felt played into the success of his practice. He didn't have the luxury of appearing bothered.

But he'd be damned if his house didn't look better than his neighbors.

Chapter 3
Early in the Morning

Anderson Sr. and Sharon normally woke around 6 AM and proceeded to get the kids ready for school. Anderson Sr. handled Andy, their ten-year-old, and Sharon handled Corliss, their seven-year-old. Both were old enough to ride the bus to school, freeing up time for the parents to get ready for their own jobs.

A fifth grader and a second grader were enough to keep their hands full, but the kids were fairly mature for their ages, *precocious* one might even say.

Saying goodbye, the kids would squirm as Sharon licked her thumb and wiped the remaining sleep from their faces.

Chapter 4
The Cabbage Patch Doll

CORLISS's wish list revolved around one thing: a Cabbage Patch doll.

"Of all the things that little girl could want," Anderson Sr. said, "she would pick the hardest toy in the world to get."

Sharon shook her head. "And that's for the white ones—which is all you're gonna find around here. You know it's gonna be hard getting a Black one."

"You wanna give your cousin Violet a call and see if they have them up there in Chicago?" he asked.

"Sure. If they do, I'll send her a check."

"Growing up, I got *fruit* for Christmas. Go figure."

Chapter 5
Mr. T

"ANDY, what do you want Santa Claus to get you for Christmas?" Mama asked.

Andy didn't even hesitate. "A Mr. T action figure!"

All those evenings of watching *The A-Team* on TV had only stoked the fire. Andy had seen Mr. T on everything from *Diff'rent Strokes* to *Rocky III*. There was no Black man tougher than Mr. T. He had muscles, gold chains, and a mohawk. It was the only logical gift for a 10-year-old Black boy.

"Give me your letter tomorrow morning."

He would write it, even though he already knew the secret: *Mama was Santa's secret helper.*

Chapter 6
The Christmas Parade

IT SEEMED as if the entire town had lined the parade route, everyone in gloves and toboggans, waving feverishly at the dressed-out cars and different marching bands playing holiday tunes.

Anderson Sr. hoisted Corliss onto his shoulders so she could see and point. Andy stood closer to the street, admiring the spectacle of lights. Sharon, with one hand on Andy's shoulder and the other one in her coat pocket, smiled and rocked back and forth to the music.

In these moments Anderson Sr. was thankful for his family, thankful for the holiday, and even, deep down, thankful for the town.

Chapter 7
Bertrice and the Christmas Parade

BERTRICE WASN'T one for Christmas parades. After all, she spent her days driving a school bus and cherished her downtime. After a full day of work, she preferred to camp out on her couch and read VC Andrews novels until she went to sleep.

Eric, her only son and a member of the 3A state championship football team, would be on the team float this year, so she'd have to make an exception.

So she put on her Santa hat and DHS sweatshirt. She would cheer for Eric along the route, but afterwards she was headed home to her books.

Chapter 8
Eric and the Christmas Parade

ERIC ENJOYED the view from the float, even though he and a few players, in an effort to look macho in the 40 degree weather, wore their jerseys with no sleeves or jackets. By the time the float hit Main Street, the teenagers were regretting their decision and huddling to preserve what little warmth they could.

Eric spotted his mother with no problem, as she waved her arms back and forth like an aircraft marshaler. He waved and blew kisses.

As the flatbed moved on, he scanned the crowd for Felicia Townsend. When he found her, he suddenly felt warm.

Chapter 9
Cymbals

JAMES DEAVENS CLANG the cymbals a hair off beat, and the drum section leader quickly gave him "the eye," before returning to their elementary jazz-like version of "Jingle Bells." The Daily High School Band had already marched through downtown and was headed for the Kroger parking lot, where the parade would conclude.

James didn't want to be there. He'd joined the band and selected what he thought would be the easiest instrument, just to have an extracurricular activity on his resume for college. The cymbals were hard—and heavy—but he did try his best, for what that was worth.

Chapter 10
Bus 45

THE SCHOOL BUSES were like refrigerators at dawn. Bertrice Smalls had to crank up bus 45 and let it run for half an hour before she started her route.

Eric had only asked for one thing for Christmas: an Atari 2600. She knew he'd reached an age where he didn't much play with G.I. Joe men anymore. Still, this video game business was more than she could handle financially.

She considered calling Eric's father to see if he'd go in half with her, but he was unreliable.

Like everything else, including the bus, she'd have to do it herself.

Chapter 11
Miss Gladys's Time to Shine

Miss Gladys loved Christmas time.

As one of the few women over the age of 40 who wasn't an usher or a stewardess, she relished being over the annual Christmas pageant at Jackson Chapel CME Church.

Last year, the pastor had sung her praises at the Christmas morning service. The other women grunted "Amen" (which they uttered to the point of meaninglessness), before rolling their eyes.

Each year she attempted to make the pageant even better, having come a long way from shepherds in bathrobes with walking sticks.

The 1983 pageant would be her best by far, she was convinced.

Chapter 12
The Nutcracker

Mrs. Berry pushed the cart containing the record player into her classroom. She quickly set up the projector and screen and got the students' attention.

"Today we're going to learn about Tchaikovsky's *Nutcracker*," she said, then started the record and the projector.

Andy stared at the images of the nutcracker leading a band of soldiers against a giant multi-headed rat king and his rodent minions. It was one of the coolest things he'd ever seen!

He couldn't wait to tell Corliss about it, but he'd make sure not to make it sound too scary. He wanted her to like it.

Chapter 13
Secret Santa, Part 1

SHARON DREW Elizabeth Rooney for the third time in five years. She disliked being a Secret Santa almost as much as she disliked the heavyset woman with the blonde bouffant wig she seemed destined to try to please. With ten people in the office, it felt like the game was somehow rigged against her.

Even worse, Elizabeth was vocal about every gift she received, normally offering a back-handed compliment. ("This is nice—for a *drugstore* perfume.")

Sharon contemplated giving her a lump of coal for Christmas this time, but then she'd never live it down.

She had to play along.

Chapter 14
Morehouse

WHAT JAMES really wanted for Christmas was an early acceptance into Morehouse College, but he wouldn't be able to apply until the following year. He wasn't on track to graduate early, so he had to bide his time.

When his mother asked him what he wanted for Christmas, he told her a Morehouse sweatshirt. It was the closest he could get to the school for the time being.

His parents attended Tougaloo College and had hoped he'd consider it, but Tougaloo was still in Mississippi, and he'd had enough of Mississippi.

He hoped Atlanta, Georgia, would one day welcome him.

Chapter 15
The Gas Station Tree

ANDERSON SR. LOADED everyone into the car and drove across town to Daniel's gas station. The old man had an array of Christmas trees already rolled up and ready to go.

The game was always the same: Daniel would point him to the scrawny trees, before Anderson Sr. added a five dollar tip to show him the best one. Daniel, relishing this exchange, always had it sitting off to the side, hidden.

Afterwards, Andy would help the men tie the tree to the top of the station wagon.

They would start trimming the tree as soon as they got home.

Chapter 16
Trimming The Tree

Anderson Sr. set the tree up in the living room, and Sharon put the Temptations' Christmas album on the turntable, while Andy uncoiled the lights and Corliss rummaged through the ornaments box.

The smell of pumpkin spice candles wafted across the room mixing with the heat provided by the small fireplace.

Andy handed the string of lights to Anderson Sr., who slowly wrapped them around the tree's branches.

Together, the Parkers placed the ornaments on those branches, careful to keep them balanced.

When they finished, Anderson Sr. hoisted Corliss onto his shoulders, and she placed the star on the tree.

Chapter 17
WWF

Arturo Fielder loved the World Wrestling Federation, better known as WWF. He couldn't get enough of Hulk Hogan, Rowdy Roddy Piper, The Iron Sheik, Andre the Giant, Big John Studd, and Junkyard Dog, best known for coming out to Queen's "Another One Bites the Dust."

His absolute favorite wrestler, though, was Jimmy "Superfly" Snuka, a Fijian wrestler known for climbing to the top rope and stretching his body like a flying squirrel as he flew across the ring and landed on his opponent, pinning him for the three-count.

When Arturo grew up, he, too, wanted to wrestle in his underwear.

Chapter 18
Lady In My Life

Eric Smalls had recorded Michael Jackson's "Lady In My Life" off WARZ 103.7 by stuffing paper into the holes on top of one of his mother's old Con Funk Shun tapes. He handed the headphones of his Walkman to Felicia. He knew she loved Michael Jackson, and since she had never heard the song before, he hoped she might think of him the next time she heard it.

"I love this!" she said, a bit too loudly.

"That's how I feel about you."

"Huh? I can't hear you." She lifted the headphones.

"I was just saying I like it, too."

Chapter 19
Date Night

ANDERSON SR. and Sharon were fortunate that Felicia Townsend was available to babysit the kids, and they were determined to make the most of their date night.

Sharon had decided on the restaurant, a seafood spot in a larger town thirty miles away. Meanwhile, Anderson Sr. was given the task of figuring out which movie they should see.

Both loved science fiction, so it was a toss up between *E. T. The Extraterrestrial* and *Return of the Jedi*.

In the end Billy Dee Williams tipped the scale. They loved the idea of seeing a suave Black man in outer space.

Chapter 20
A Black President

ROBERT DEAVENS HAD GOTTEN word through some of his kinfolk in Chicago that Jesse Jackson, the reverend who was on the balcony when King was assassinated, was gearing up for a run for president of the United States. There was a part of him that knew Jesse wouldn't be able to beat Reagan, but still it was good to see another Black person aiming for the highest position in the land.

Roughly eleven years earlier, he had gone down to polls to vote for Shirley Chisholm.

Maybe one day a Black person *would* become president, hopefully in his own lifetime.

Chapter 21
Felicia

THERE WERE ONLY two things Eric thought about all day: an Atari 2600 and Felicia. He had no control over whether he could get the former (although he pleaded with his mother to get him one for Christmas), but he felt he had at least a passing chance at gaining Felicia's affections.

The two had been friends since kindergarten, and there had been moments when a glance seemed to linger between them. Eric hoped that maybe there was something in that glance.

Maybe he needed a Jheri curl like Michael Jackson.

He wondered if Ma would let him get one.

Chapter 22
Corliss's Toys

EVEN THOUGH CORLISS shared a bedroom with her older brother, she found a way to populate her space with an array of Monchichis and Smurfs and, if Santa got her what she wished for, a Cabbage Patch doll.

She loved the little world she'd created for herself, often times setting up her toys for tea parties or having them serve as a buffer around her when she slept—just in case any boogey men made it past her big brother. They were her army, just like the wooden soldiers in *The Nutcracker*, and they would defend the Parkers' house valiantly.

Chapter 23
The Color of Santa

Sharon was Santa's helper. That was the official story that she'd produced in reaction to Corliss's persistent questions about the old man.

"Is Santa Claus a white man?" she'd added.

Andy had had similar questions when he was her age, and Sharon had almost botched that one, but in this rare moment of genius, she responded, "He becomes the color of the family inside the household."

The logic of this could easily be surmounted by an older kid, especially if there were multiple races in a single household, but it seemed to satisfy Corliss's six-year-old mind.

"Mommy, that's pretty cool!"

Chapter 24
No Dripping

"No," Bertrice told her son. "There is no way I'm letting you get a curl. The activator gets on everything and stains it."

"But, Ma," Eric said, "everyone has one—even Michael Jackson!"

"If everyone jumped off a cliff, would you?"

She always said this, and she knew that it would normally shut down the discussion.

"Maybe."

Bertrice eyed her son carefully. "Some little girl done got your nose wide open, I'm guessing."

He looked away.

"Baby, you're a handsome young man already. You don't need to change yourself to make someone like you."

He smiled and reluctantly hugged her.

Chapter 25
TV Night

SHARON PUT the popcorn kernels into a sauce pan on the stove, and Anderson Sr. adjusted the antennae on top of the television (which was on top of a larger floor model television that didn't work any longer and served as furniture).

Andy and Corliss grabbed the afghan their maternal grandmother had knitted for them and snuggled up on the couch.

Once the popcorn was ready and the channel was clear, the Parkers would sit down and watch *A Charlie Brown Christmas* or *Frosty the Snowman* or *Rudolph the Red-Nosed Reindeer*.

Afterwards, the parents would sleep better than the kids.

Chapter 26
Please, Let It Snow

ON THE NIGHT before the last day of school gave way to the winter break, Andy prayed for snow.

Mississippi could get pretty cold in December, with the pipes sometimes freezing because the ground had turned into a tundra, but there was rarely a good snowfall to bring in the Christmas season.

Corliss slept, clutching her teddy bear, on the opposite side of the room in her portion of the disassembled bunk beds. Anderson wondered if she'd prayed for snow, too. She normally got what she wanted.

He fell asleep, hoping for a thick layer of snow in the morning.

Chapter 27
Snow

THE SNOW DRIFTED SOFTLY at first and then quickly picked up until it was nearly blinding. Andy could hardly sit still.

And all of it was sticking to the ground!

After lunch, the principal announced school would be closing early, effectively starting the winter break two hours early.

Andy didn't know what he was going to do first: make snow angels, roll up snowballs, or build a snowman.

Surely there was an epic neighborhood snowball fight awaiting him when he got home from school.

A white Christmas at last!

He knew he would have to thank Corliss for this one.

Chapter 28
The Latchkey Kids

CORLISS BOARDED bus 45 and headed to sit next to her older brother. "We got snow!" she sang.

"I know! Isn't it great?" Andy said.

"Can we play in the snow when we get home?"

"I don't see why not."

Andy felt for the house key affixed to a cord that slid beneath his cable sweater.

Now that he was ten, his parents were comfortable with him being a latchkey kid. His only responsibility was to not let in strangers and to take care of Corliss.

Surely, he could hold down the fort—even with the snow—until five o'clock.

Chapter 29
The Deavens Kids

AMBER DEAVENS COULD SEE the kids in the neighborhood gathering in the street. Andy and Corliss had just come outdoors, so maybe her big brother, James, would let her go outside, too. After all, with school being out, she didn't really have any homework.

James, a 10th grade honor roll student with his sights set on Morehouse, was relentless in pushing her so she could get accepted into Spelman one day.

"Fine," he said, "but make sure you do some reading when you come in."

She knew he wouldn't join her, so she didn't ask.

He wasn't built that way.

Chapter 30
The Snowball War, Part 1

ARTURO THREW THE FIRST SNOWBALL—AND it hit Nelson Griggs in the forehead.

Andy was the first to retaliate, his perfectly shaped snowball firing through the air as if it were thrown by Satchel Paige himself.

Nelson quickly collected himself and joined in.

After the first few snowballs had been thrown, the kids from around the block quickly picked sides and joined in, everyone laughing and slinging snow.

Big Frank, a husky kid from two streets over hurled a misshapen snowball that exploded against the windshield of Evan Thomas's Cadillac. Suddenly everything got deathly quiet.

Evan's front door opened slowly.

Chapter 31
The Snowball War, Part 2

"Who hit my car?" Evan yelled, his voice much higher than even he expected it to be.

No one said a thing.

"So I'm going to have to mess all of you kids up then?"

Suddenly a snowball went sailing through the air, smacking him in his chest.

"So that's how we're doing it?" Evan said, turning around and grabbing his overcoat from the foyer.

He quickly scooped up snow from his steps before the neighborhood kids could run and started dropping bombs.

The kids laughed, as did Evan, and the grown-ups gradually joined in, rounding out the snowball war.

Chapter 32
The Snowman

CORLISS HAD ALREADY STARTED on the snowman in the Parker's front yard when Amber walked across the street to join her.

"You need help?" Amber asked.

Corliss smiled, nodding. "Sure!"

The neighborhood boys (along with a few adults) hurled snowballs at each other up and down Elm Street, while Corliss and Amber remained safely insulated from the chaos.

"You know what the key to an amazing snowman is?" Amber asked.

Corliss nodded. "A carrot nose."

"Let's see if we can find a stick that looks like a carrot."

That day the two girls built the best snowman in the neighborhood.

Chapter 33
A Phone Call

ERIC DIALED Felicia's phone number and stretched the telephone cord into the bathroom, where he closed the door for privacy.

"Hello," she answered softly.

Eric lowered his voice as best he could before answering. "May I speak to Felicia?"

"This is she."

"Hey, this is Eric."

"Hi, Eric. How'd you get my number?"

"The phone book," he responded, without even thinking of how embarrassing an admission that was.

"So what's up?" she said.

He didn't know what to say. He honestly hadn't expected to get this far.

He took a deep breath before responding, "I was just thinking about you…."

Chapter 34
Pageant Patience

JACKSON CHAPEL WAS ALREADY a small church with a handful of children, but the situation facing Miss Gladys didn't make much sense.

The Smith kids were headed to St. Louis to visit family for Christmas. The Robinsons were headed to see their grandparents in Detroit. The Williamses were headed to Atlanta with their father. That left only the Parkers.

She had no idea how to do a pageant with only two people. Still, she could hear the women in the church whispering their schadenfreude.

She'd have to push ahead, even if it was just Andy and Corliss playing every part.

Chapter 35
The First Date

THEY'D AGREED to meet at the gazebo in the park downtown, amid the festive arrangements. The bench next to the gazebo's railing was the only place not completely covered in snow.

Eric brought a blanket, two mugs, and a thermos of hot chocolate.

He and Felicia snuggled together as streetlights, interlaced with Christmas lights, glowed around them.

"So what did you ask Santa to bring you for Christmas?" she said with a smile.

It was a cute question that sounded even cuter coming from her lips.

He slowly placed his arm around her shoulder.

"I asked him for this moment."

Chapter 36
Brown Faces

IN HER QUEST TO make the Christmas season feel magical for her family, Sharon decided to buy an array of holiday figurines to place on the shelves and over the mantle of the fireplace. Every single character in the store was white, so she bought brown magic markers and took the figurines home to work on them.

With the kids buzzing in and out of the room, she carefully colored the faces and hands of each character. One by one, the figurines began to resemble her own family.

It was important that the kids saw themselves represented in the season.

Chapter 37
Two Brothers

BERTRICE OFTEN DID her best to avoid calling her little brother, Ray Ray, for favors, but he was the only person she could think of who might help her.

Ironically, her older brother, Kevin, a sheriff's deputy, was the fiscally-responsible straight arrow who always did things by the book. Ray Ray, on the other hand, was quietly known to procure certain things at a lower price.

Bertrice had begun to reach a point where she cared less and less about the gaming system's origins. She just wanted to give her son a good Christmas.

She decided to pray on it.

Chapter 38
The Last One

ANDY AND CORLISS begged their mother to push the shopping cart through the toy section of the department store.

"We're not buying toys today," Sharon said.

"We know. We just want to *see* them."

While Sharon took Corliss around to a spot where the Cabbage Patch dolls would have been (if they'd had them), Andy quickly made a bee-line for the action figures.

There was one Mr. T on the shelf.

If Sharon didn't get it, then someone else would! (*The agony!*)

He grabbed it. "Look, Mama! It's the only one."

She nodded and told him to put it back.

Chapter 39
The Lights of the Tree

SHORTLY AFTER DINNER, Andy curled up on the floor in the darkened living room, staring up at the lights of the tree. The glow of it was magical and reminded him of the decorated trees in department stores and at school, except this tree was *better*.

Sharon had already started putting presents beneath it, and while there were only two for him right now (both too large and flat to be a Mr. T action figure), he loved the look of it all.

He didn't even realize that he'd fallen asleep until his father woke him.

"Time for bed, tiger."

Chapter 40
Ray Ray's Dilemma

Ray Ray Smalls had never seen the inside of a jail. Whether it was good luck or the fact that his brother intentionally ignored what amounted to a little "harmless" fencing of goods of indiscernible origins, he couldn't tell.

"It would break Mom and Dad's hearts if they knew you were out here in the streets like this," Kevin had told him once.

He wanted to stop, but there was nothing else he was good at. He wasn't the 9-to-5 type.

He wanted to do the right thing and be a credit to his family. He just didn't know how.

Chapter 41
Help Wanted

THE "HELP WANTED" sign Robert Deavens posted in the window of his bicycle shop had only been affixed to the window for five minutes before Ray Ray bounded in asking for an application.

Robert knew the Smalls family fairly well, hard-working people they were, but he didn't know much about Ray Ray.

"Know anything about bikes?" Robert asked.

"Not as much as I could know if you *taught* me," Ray Ray responded.

For some reason, the answer hit home. The young man really wanted to learn.

It was the Christmas season. Maybe Robert would give this guy a chance.

Chapter 42
Smile

ANDERSON SR. first learned about the new organization through his dental trade journals. As an American dentist, he didn't spend much time thinking about cleft palates, as they were usually corrected through surgery during infancy using a procedure called palatoplasty.

Maybe it was the Christmas season that gave him pause, made him understand he had to do what he could to help other people, in whatever way he could. As a family dentist, he wouldn't be performing any surgeries; still, he could see many uses for a good dentist.

That morning during his break, he reached out to Operation Smile.

Chapter 43
Secret Santa, Part 2

Elizabeth Rooney was the third person to open her gift. This year Sharon opted to go with a snow globe that contained a fat little cherub that could've very well been related to Elizabeth.

At first Elizabeth stared at it curiously, then quickly announced, "I think this is the best gift I've ever received from work!"

Sharon tried not to seem pleased, but she couldn't help herself. It was her turn to go next.

She peeled back the wrapping paper to reveal the very same perfume she'd gifted Elizabeth last year.

Biting her lip, she sighed and said, "Thank you."

Chapter 44
The Cabbage Patch Doll From Chicago

SHARON'S COUSIN Violet had been able to come through with a Black Cabbage Patch doll. To hear Violet tell it, she'd had to engage in a few transactions that led to the scoring of the doll. Sharon wasn't sure she wanted to know anything further. She was simply happy that she and Anderson Sr. would be able to give Corliss what she wanted for Christmas.

The doll arrived in a large box, and Sharon quickly wrapped it and placed it under the tree.

When she finally got around to Andy's gift, the store had already sold out of action figures.

Chapter 45
The MJ Mixtape

With the relationship still fresh, Eric had no idea of what to give Felicia for Christmas. His funds running low, he decided to go through his mother's records and find as many slow jams by Michael Jackson as he could, everything from *Thriller* and *Off the Wall*, as well as some old Motown cuts.

Eric patiently created a mixtape and designed the artwork by creating a collage of images cobbled together from the old *Jet* magazines stacked in the corner of the bathroom.

He wrapped it and stuck a bow on top.

Felicia smiled as if he'd given her diamonds.

The Best Christmas Pageant Ever?

MISS GLADYS WAS FLIPPING channels and serendipitously came across a television program called *The Best Christmas Pageant Ever*, based off the children's book of the same name by Barbara Robinson.

The Herdmans had been corralled into making the best pageant the town had ever seen, after having bullied their way to the best spots.

Miss Gladys may've had only two children with whom to work, but at least there was one boy and one girl. That was enough for a Mary and a Joseph, and neither kid was anything like the Herdmans, so she figured it might all work out.

Chapter 47
Two Brothers and a Sister

WHEN RAY RAY and Kevin pulled up—together—Bertrice feared the worst. After the passing of their parents, the siblings were rarely in the same space, even during the holidays.

Had something happened to Eric?

Kevin popped the trunk and removed a large wrapped box.

"Is *that* what I think it is?" she asked, trying to steady herself.

"We just thought the boy needed to have a good Christmas," Kevin said.

Ray Ray added, "We went in half and half on an Atari for him."

Unable to hold back her tears, Bertrice collapsed into her brothers' embraces, thankful for family.

Chapter 48
Jive Turkey

BECAUSE SHARON WORKED in the mayor's office, she could always count on the main part of the Parker Christmas dinner being free: the turkey.

Mayor McFarland insisted on giving all employees of City Hall a hefty bird, frozen all the way through, which he handed out to them, a Santa hat sitting on his head.

In some ways Sharon viewed it as patronizing, but a free turkey was nothing to sneeze at, especially when you had a household of four who would eat that bird baked, fried, stuffed, marinated in gravy, or sliced.

Her pride could definitely take the hit.

Chapter 49
The Mall Santa Claus

DAILY WAS TOO small to have a mall, so the Parkers drove forty miles to Tupelo so the kids could sit on Santa's knee and tell them what they wanted for Christmas. Sharon and Anderson Sr. had debated if they should let their children believe their gifts came from a heavyset white man wearing red. Sharon convinced him it would be harmless.

A few years earlier Corliss had peed all over Santa's leg when it was her turn. Anderson Sr. had to bite his inner cheeks to keep from smiling.

The trip had grown into a tradition, sans the urine.

Chapter 50
Kwanzaa

"I THINK we're gonna try it this year," Anderson Sr. said.

"We've been doing it for two years now." Robert Deavens leaned back proudly.

"Sharon's open to it, but we both keep messing up the pronunciations of the days. We don't want to look like complete idiots to our kids."

Robert nodded. "Been there, done that."

"I just want the kids to know they have their own culture, too. Know what I'm saying?"

"Andy, you're preaching to the choir. Who knows? Maybe in thirty years it'll be as big as Christmas."

Anderson Sr. nodded slowly, though he seriously doubted that.

Chapter 51
The Jackson Chapel CME
Church Christmas Pageant

Miss Gladys turned out the lights over the pulpit and read the scripture in her best diction.

The Angel of the Lord (Corliss) appeared at the back of the sanctuary, white robe, halo, and wings. "Unto you a child is born," she said, working the aisle like a runway.

Andy appeared in a kingly robe carrying frankincense. Then, through a trick of strobe lights, he switched to myrrh, then gold, appearing to be three different people.

Finally, the sanctuary went dark and a spotlight shone on Joseph (Andy) and Mary (Corliss), a baby doll swaddled between them.

It was perfect!

Chapter 52
The Salvation Army Bell

BECAUSE ANDERSON SR. and Sharon were in a constitutionally-bound fraternity and sorority, they took the kids out each year to ring the Salvation Army bell in front of Wal-Mart with their organizations.

Jesse Weatherspoon always dressed in a royal blue Santa costume and held the main bell, while Andy and Corliss led the group in songs that many of the members had forgotten over the years.

The group closed with a rambunctious version of "Jingle Bells," pausing intermittently to thank donors who dropped folded cash into the big red kettle.

Afterwards, the Parkers would head home and make hot chocolate.

Chapter 53
Jesse Pitches Woo to Bertrice

BERTRICE SPOTTED Jesse Weatherspoon stepping out of his UPS truck holding a package.

"Ma'am, can you sign for this?"

"Do you see a *ma'am* anywhere out here?" she responded, taking the pen from him.

"Actually, no disrespect to your husband, but you're a sight for sore eyes."

"He doesn't mind—since he doesn't exist," she said, laughing.

"Well, this must be my lucky day. Can I get your number?"

"That's kinda forward, ain't it?"

"I'm a man who knows what he wants."

"Maybe next time," she said, struggling to contain her smile.

He winked and walked back to his truck.

Chapter 54
The Night Before Christmas

ANDY TOSSED and turned in his twin bed, while Corliss tossed and turned in hers. Neither could get to sleep.

"Do you think Santa's on his way here?" she whispered.

"I think so, but Mama said he wouldn't come until he knew for sure that we were asleep."

"But I can't sleep."

"Neither can I."

"I wonder if we'll hear the reindeer on the roof," Corliss said.

Andy had never considered that. "Maybe."

They tossed and turned for a few more minutes.

"Can you tell me the story of the little girl and the nutcracker again?" Corliss whispered drowsily.

"Sure."

Chapter 55
Corliss Welcomes Adrienne

THE SUN HAD BARELY RISEN when Corliss leaped from her bed and shook her older brother awake.

"It's Christmas!" she yelled, sounding the alarm for the entire household to wake up.

The kids ran into the living room, followed by their parents wiping sleep from their eyes.

Corliss dove for the big box with her name on it and started ripping off the colorful wrapping paper.

"A Cabbage Patch doll!" she gushed. "And it says here her name is Adrienne Dorine. Welcome to the Parkers' house, Adrienne Dorine!"

Her parents stood by smiling, silently high-fiving themselves for this small victory.

Chapter 56
Andy's Last Gift

AFTER ANDY OPENED all of his gifts under the tree, his disappointment was palpable. There was no Mr. T action figure.

Sharon felt her heart drop. She'd waited too late and when she returned to the store, it was already gone. "Hey, let's be thankful for the gifts we received. There are many people who didn't get a thing."

Andy nodded. "Yes, ma'am."

"Did you check over there behind the couch?" Anderson Sr. said.

Andy quickly ran over and discovered a package with his name on it. He tore it open and screamed in triumph.

Anderson Sr. winked at Sharon.

<h1 style="text-align:center">Chapter 57
How Chitterlings Become
Chitlins</h1>

First, Sharon would thaw them out. Once they were manageable, she'd pull the fat off of them, a feat that required a level of meticulousness not often found in the Parker kitchen. She then added them to the pot and put in some onions ("to break up the smell," she sometimes said), before putting on the lid and letting them cook. Sometimes she would fry some of them afterwards, since Anderson Sr. liked them that way.

Andy loved them, but Corliss hated them.

"How could you love something so stinky?" she'd ask.

"They're only stinky if you don't love them."

Chapter 58
Mario Brothers

THE SMALLS FAMILY launched the first ever *Mario Brothers* tournament right after Christmas dinner. With Eric feverishly working the joystick, Kevin and Ray-Ray debated who'd been the better player on the *Donkey Kong* arcade game that gave way to this sequel.

"Well, it doesn't matter which of you was better," Bertrice said, laughing, "'cause I got *next!*"

The brothers laughed. Then everyone turned their attention to Eric, who was now navigating the Italian plumber through another maze.

Bertrice had already thanked her brothers repeatedly for coming through for her and Eric, but she was even more thankful for this moment.

Chapter 59
The Christmas Picture

THE DEAVENS FAMILY piled into their brand new minivan, a vehicle that Doris felt her husband had paid a little too much for, trying to keep up with the "Joneses."

James and Amber loved the Christmas lights, almost as much as Robert and Doris, so they took their time cruising through the town, taking in the sights.

Daily was a beautiful town at Christmas time, and the Deavens, above everyone, appreciated every little detail.

Finally, they found their way to the gazebo in the park. Beneath a street lamp, Robert balanced his Polaroid and took their annual family Christmas picture.

Chapter 60
And to All a Good Night

ANDY AND CORLISS fell asleep at the base of the Christmas tree, while Anderson Sr. and Sharon sat on the couch, fingers intertwined, listening to Donny Hathaway's "This Christmas."

"Good job, Mrs. Claus," Anderson Sr. whispered.

"Good job, Mr. Claus," Sharon responded, snuggling closer to him.

They knew their Christmases wouldn't always be like this. The children would get older, and the traditions would evolve into something different. But in this moment, they were the proud parents of two wonderful children, and life was good.

They would cherish the Christmas of 1983 and hold those memories for years to come.

Acknowledgments

First, I'd like to thank my wife and daughter for all of their love and support. This project would have been impossible without their encouragement.

I'd also like to thank my parents and my brother for a childhood full of love and wonder.

Thank you to my extended family and in-laws for your continued love and support.

Special thanks to the Dumas Collective (Sabin, Van, and Chris).

Shout out to Grant Faulkner for the assist on locking down the title.

Also, thanks to the following people: Scott Semegran, Richard Wall, Laurie Carter, Mitchell Davis and the BiblioLabs team, Kelvin Watson, Denise Raleigh, Jane Friedman, L. Penelope, Maurice Carlos Ruffin, Rion Amilcar Scott, the James River Writers, Kima Jones, the staff of the William R. and Norma B. Harvey Library at Hampton University, my creative writing students, Amy Jones and the *Writer's Digest* team, Guy Gonzalez, Dr. William R. Harvey, and the many people who have supported me throughout the years. Please charge it to my head and not my heart that your names are not individually listed here.

About the Author

Ran Walker is the author of twenty-eight books. He is the winner of the Indie Author Project's 2019 Indie Author of the Year Award, the 2019 Black Caucus of the ALA Fiction Ebook Award, the 2018 Virginia Author Project Award for Adult Fiction, and the 2021 Blind Corner Afrofuturism Microfiction Award. He teaches creative writing at Hampton University and at Writer's Digest University and lives with his wife and daughter in Virginia. He can be reached via his website, www.ranwalker.com.

Also by Ran Walker

B-Sides and Remixes

30 Love: A Novel

Mojo's Guitar: A Novel/ (Il était une fois Morris Jones)

Afro Nerd in Love: A Novella

The Keys of My Soul: A Novel

The Race of Races: A Novel

The Illest: A Novella

Bessie, Bop, or Bach: Collected Stories

Four Floors (with Sabin Prentis)

Black Hand Side: Stories

White Pages: A Novel

She Lives in My Lap

Reverb

Work-In-Progress

Daykeeper

Most of My Heroes Don't Appear On No Stamps

Portable Black Magic

The Strange Museum: 50-Word Stories

Bees + Things + Flowers: Microfictions

The World Is Yours: Microfictions

Can I Kick It?: Sneaker Microfiction and Poetry

The Golden Book: A 50-Year Marriage Told In 50-Word Stories

Keep It 100: 100-Word Stories

A Burst of Gray: A Novel In 100-Word Stories

The Library of Afro Curiosities: 100-Word Stories

Black Marker: And Other 100-Word Stories

The Adventures of GloKat: A Novel in 100-Word Stories

www.ingramcontent.com/pod-product-compliance
Lightning Source LLC
Chambersburg PA
CBHW042033120726
47911CB00026B/728